For Janice Thomson –
thanks for everything, Wise Owl.
J.W. and T.R.

Text copyright © Jeanne Willis, 2006. Illustrations copyright © Tony Ross, 2006.
The rights of Jeanne Willis and Tony Ross to be identified as the author and illustrator of this
work have been asserted by them in accordance with the Copyright, Designs and Patents Act, 1988.
First published in Great Britain in 2006 by Andersen Press Ltd., 20 Vauxhall Bridge Road, London SW1V 2SA.
Published in Australia by Random House Australia Pty., 20 Alfred Street, Milsons Point, Sydney, NSW 2061.
All rights reserved. Colour separated in Switzerland by Photolitho AG, Zürich.
Printed and bound in Italy by Grafiche AZ, Verona.

10   9   8   7   6   5   4   3   2   1

British Library Cataloguing in Publication Data available.

ISBN-10: 1 84270 476 1
ISBN-13: 978 1 84270 476 9

This book has been printed on acid-free paper

DAFT BAT

Jeanne Willis and Tony Ross

Andersen Press • London

There was once a bat who got everything round the wrong way.

At least, that's what the wild, young animals thought.

It all started when Bat first arrived.

Wise Owl wanted to give her a Welcome Gift, so he asked the wild, young animals to go and find out what she would like.

"I'd like an umbrella to keep my feet dry, please," she said.

"Umbrellas keep *heads* dry, not feet!"
whispered Baby Elephant. "Daft old Bat!"

"Anyone can make a mistake," said Goat Kid.

So they thought no more about it and gave her a smart new umbrella.

But then Bat said another very odd thing.

She said, "I'm so glad you brought me an umbrella.
There's a big, black rain cloud in the sky below."

"Daft old Bat!" giggled Giraffe Calf.
"The sky is *above*, not below!"

And then Bat said another funny thing.

"If it rains very hard the river will rise and my ears will get wet," she said.

"But if the river rises our *toes* will get wet, not our ears!" growled Lion Cub.

"I would wear a rain hat, but it would only fall off into the grass above," Bat added.

"But the grass isn't above, it's *below!*" muttered Rhino Junior. "What a daft old bat she is!"

By now, all the wild, young animals thought Bat was completely barmy.

So they ran off to tell Wise Owl.

"Bat's bonkers! She's barking mad!" said Baby Elephant.
"If she's mad, she might be dangerous!" said Lion Cub.
"Help!" said Goat Kid.

"Why do you think Bat is mad?" hooted Owl.

"She sees things differently to us," said Rhino Junior.
"Very differently," said Giraffe Calf.

Owl looked thoughtful. Then he said, "I will ask Bat some simple questions and I will decide if anyone needs their head examining."

So they all went to visit Bat. Owl asked if she would mind answering a few questions. "Not at all," she said.

"Question Number One," said Owl. "What does a tree look like?"

"That's easy," said Bat, "A tree has a trunk at the top and leaves at the bottom."

"See, Owl? Bat *is* daft!" laughed Giraffe Calf. "A tree has a trunk at the *bottom* and leaves at the *top*. Even I know that!"

"Question Number Two!" said Owl. "What does a mountain look like?"

"That's even easier!" said Bat. "A mountain has a flat bit at the top and a pointy bit hanging down."

"You daft old bat! The pointy bit of a mountain sticks *up*, not down!" said Goat Kid. "I know, I'm a mountain goat."
"Bat is mad!" they all cried. "Call the doctor!"

"Last question!" said Owl. "And I'd like everyone to answer it, except Bat."
"All right," said the wild, young animals.
"What's the question?"

And Wise Owl said, "Question Number Three! Have you ever tried looking at things from *Bat's* point of view?"

And he made them all hang upside down from
a branch – just like her.

"Oooh," said Goat Kid. "Bat was right! When you look at it
like this, the pointy bit of the mountain does hang down!"
"And the tree has a trunk at the *top* and leaves at the
bottom," said Giraffe Calf.

"And the sky . . . isn't!"

"Heeey! The grass is *above* our heads!" said Rhino Junior.

Just then it started to rain. It rained and rained and it rained.

"Can I get down now, Owl? The river is rising.
My ears are wet!" said Lion Cub.
"And my feet are getting soaked from this angle!"
said Baby Elephant.

So Bat lent him her smart new umbrella to keep them dry.

"Thank you," he said. "I'm so sorry I said you were mad."
"We're all sorry," said the wild, young animals.

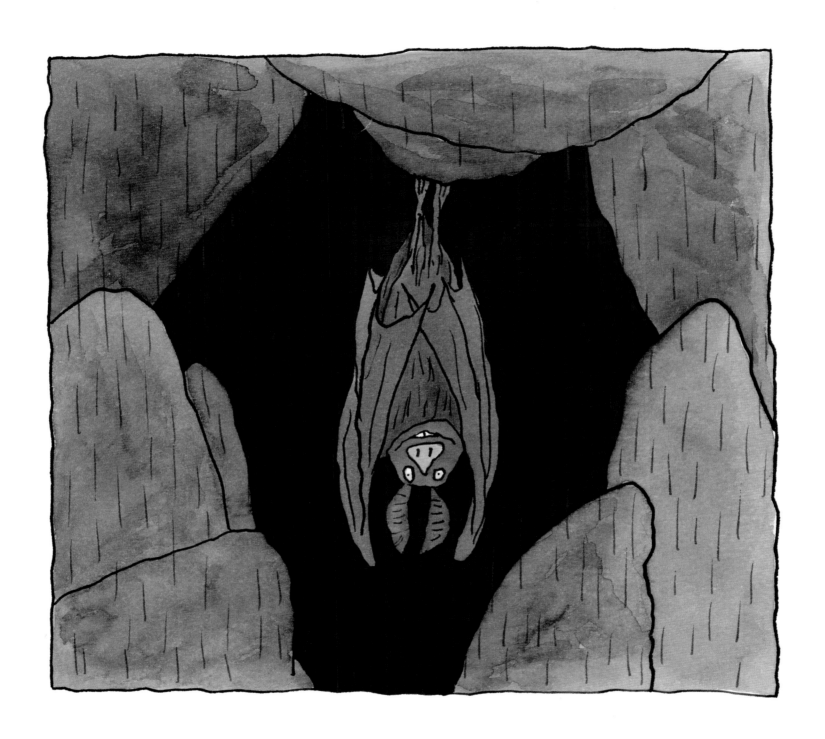

"Oh . . . don't be daft!" smiled Bat.

Other titles from Jeanne Willis and Tony Ross:

"One of the classic picture book partnerships" Achuka

I Hate School

Killer Gorilla

Manky Monkey

Misery Moo

Really Rude Rhino

Shhh!

Tadpole's Promise